Agi and the Thought Compass
by Betsy O'Neill-Sheehan
Illustrated by Manuel Herrera
Published by EduMatch®
PO Box 150324, Alexandria, VA 22315

www.edumatch.org

ISBN-10: 978-1-970133-90-5

A Special Note for Families and Educators

Welcome to this book! Before you go on with your child, I want to tell you how it works. This is an introduction to cognitive self-awareness: noticing how our thoughts impact how we feel and what we do. Thoughts are powerful. Many effective therapies teach people how to guide and rephrase their thoughts to more helpful ones. I have seen that when we introduce these strategies to children early in life, they have a better understanding of their own cognitions, and feel empowered and autonomous in their choices and feelings. After reading the story, try exploring with some of these strategies together:

Thought Compass: If we think of our imagination as an inner world, it can get scattered and overwhelming without some sort of direction. Craft a real thought compass together as a tool to experiment with. When your child expresses a thought, ask where the compass arrow is pointing. (Is it real or imagined? Helpful or not?) Let your child experiment and play with it. In time they will develop their own internal compass.

Thought Mapping: Help your child visualize and sketch their thoughts on a thought map. Guide, but let them decide where on the map the thoughts they express are located. This is an engaging way to graphically organize and communicate the inner world. Get creative, make, & play!

Imagined & Unhelpful: Untrue negative self-talk, spiralling worry thoughts, impulsive angry thoughts.	**Imagined & Helpful:** pretend play, inventing, exploring, creating, making.
Real & Not helpful: Real thoughts become unhelpful when they trigger negative self-talk or self-esteem. They can also be unhelpful if we don't take care of them or ask for help.	**Real & Helpful:** Mindful of the moment that you are in. Real thoughts can also be helpful when they signal that we need to ask for help with something.

For more discussion questions and activities, please visit my website at www.betsyoneillsheehan.com.

From Betsy:
For Rob, Bobby, Liam, Ceallach
& All of Our Family
We all get a little lost sometimes.

And for the Blais Family,
Who know the true strength of Imagination.

From Manuel::
To my mother, Mary.
Thank you for always encouraging me to draw and
create art. I love you.

When you have a world so big
inside your head,

it's easy to get
lost.

Sometimes it feels like my thoughts are
planted on the ground.

I **see** what is **real**.

I **feel** what is **real**.

Other times I feel my thoughts floating away.

In my imagination,

I can travel on exciting adventures,

— I DID IT!

dream of my future,

CALIFORNIA HERE WE COME!

or visit fond memories.

But sometimes I **think** the **worst.**

I **see** the **worst.**

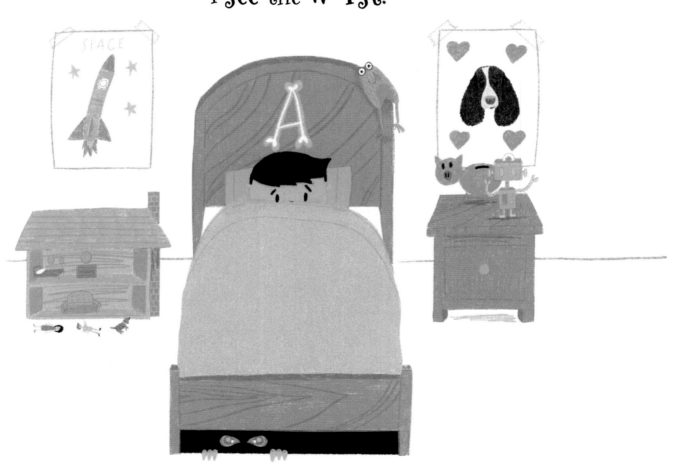

I **feel** the **worst.**

My imagination spins

out of control.

When my parents saw the whirl I was in,
they took me to Scoops to meet a new friend.
They said, "Sometimes it's good to share your thoughts,
look at things differently, and learn the strengths you've got."

"I'm Agi Nation," I told him,
"Sometimes I get lost in my **imagination**."

"I'm Blais, a thought trainer," he said. "Knowing you
are lost is the first step in finding your way back.."

"How did you become a thought trainer?" I asked.

"Well, it took some practice and it took some time,
but I can try anything
when I wonder in my mind...

I imagine:

running,

playing,

flying.

I can even make myself a superhero, the bravest and funniest kind."

"Sometimes my thoughts make me feel worried, angry, or sad.
I listen, then steer them to more helpful ones that I have.

I use my thought compass. Want to try it?" he asked.

"I do!"

"Hold it in your hand and you'll learn to control
and guide your thoughts where you want them to go.

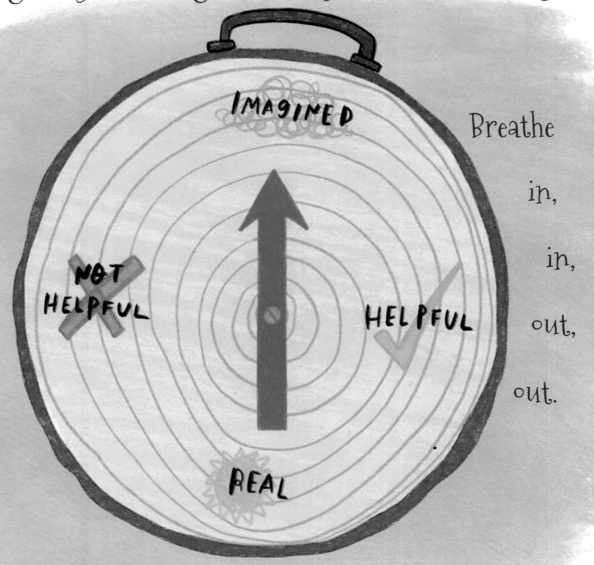

Breathe

in,

in,

out,

out.

Start here to calm your big feelings down."

"Then find where you are in the thought you are in.

Is it real or imagined? Is it helpful or not?

Once you know where you are
you can plan your way out."

"Find three things around you that are real in your space.
Look around you.
What is real? What do you see?
Smell? Feel? Taste?

Where are your thoughts now?"
Blais asked.

I felt it come in like a dark summer storm.

I got so lost in thought I forgot how to talk.

Then I heard Blais's voice echo on the wind,

"You have the control!

Tell your thoughts where you want them to go!"

Remembering the compass I had in my hand,

I blew the wind in, in, out, out ...
until I felt the storm calm down.

"This thought is **unhelpful**, it is **not real!**
I control my thoughts! I control how I feel!"

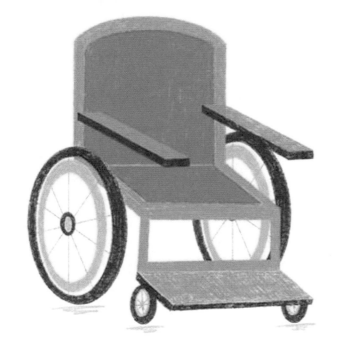

Then I saw his wheelchair,

then his green
shirt,

then his face,

and I felt the comfort of a friend who was real in my space.

"Agi, you did it!" said Blais.

"You used your thought compass!
Practice and **you** will guide your **imagination**."

I keep my compass handy to navigate the mysteries in my mind.

Sometimes I let myself get a little lost,

but I know how to find my way out.

I'm Agi Nation
and my **imagination**
is me.

Sometimes I wander in wonder, but now
I control what I think.

Betsy is an elementary school counselor bridging traditional counseling with current technologies. She is often confused for a unicorn and may potentially be carrying a thought compass on her person. A mother of three and SEL educator, she knows there is no substitute for connections children make through stories and play. In 2019 she was recognized as a Pioneer Valley Educator of Excellence. You can find her on Twitter @eoneillsheehan, her website at betsyoneillsheehan.com, or running through her hometown of East Longmeadow, MA.

For more THOUGHT COMPASS & MAPPING Activities follow this link:

Manuel is an educator, a speaker, and an illustrator. Most importantly, he is a father of two young boys. Over the past 18 years of his career, he has keynoted and led workshops at educational conferences across the country. Manuel has illustrated books, publications, and graphics for a variety of organizations, businesses, and schools. Currently, he is the Coordinator of Learning Services for the Affton School District and an adjunct professor for Webster University. Both located in St. Louis, MO. You can follow Manuel on Twitter and Instagram at @manuelherrera33.

EduMatch Publishing

Made in the USA
Monee, IL
03 October 2020